The TRUTH
According to Arthur

Tim HOPGOOD

David TAZZYMAN

BLOOMSBURY
LONDON OXFORD NEW YORK NEW DELHI SYDNEY

This is
Arthur.

And this is
The Truth.

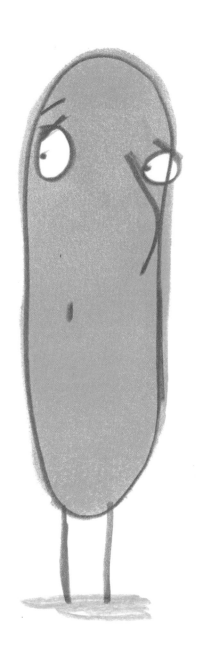

Arthur and The Truth
are **NOT** the best of
friends right now . . .

because
today THIS
happened,

which caused THIS . . .

...and also

THIS!

The Truth was, Arthur knew he'd done **WRONG** because his mum had told him he **wasn't** to ride his brother's **BIG** bike.

So when his friend Noah
asked what had happened,
Arthur tried
BENDING
The Truth
just a little bit.

"This supercool princess asked
if she could have a go on
my brother's bike.

She'd never ridden one before . . .

. . . and bashed into my mum's car.
She didn't even say
SOrry!"

"**Uh-oh!**
I bet your mum's going
to be **REALLY** cross,"
said Noah.

That wasn't **EXACTLY** what Arthur wanted to hear.

So when his friend Lula asked him
what had happened, Arthur tried
STRETCHING
The Truth instead.

"I was just having a little go on my brother's bike when an **alien** asked if he could borrow it.

He said he needed it to get home . . .

". . . I think he thought it would fly!"

"Uh-oh!
I bet your mum's NOT
going to be very pleased!"
sighed Lula.

That wasn't EXACTLY
what Arthur wanted
to hear either.

Arthur decided that more drastic
action was needed.

He tried COVERING UP

The Truth . . .

DISGUISING it . . .

HIDING it . . .

but it refused to stay covered up,
or disguised, or hidden!

So when Little Frankie asked Arthur
what had happened,

Arthur decided just to **I**

G

N The Truth

O altogether.

R

E

"It has NOTHING to do with me.
My brother's bike just transformed into a

Giant Robot

and Mum's car did too.

There was a
HUGE
fight ...

. . . and Mum's car won!"

"Cooool!" said Little Frankie.
"I bet your mum WILL be
pleased about that."

"Err, I hope so,"
said Arthur.

"Arthur!"

It was Mum.

Time for Arthur to face The Truth.
He looked The Truth square in the eye.
The Truth looked back.

"Arthur, do you have
something to tell me?"

asked his mum.

What will **Arthur** do?

What would **YOU** do?

Well, Arthur said something
that **surprised** even him . . .

"It was me!

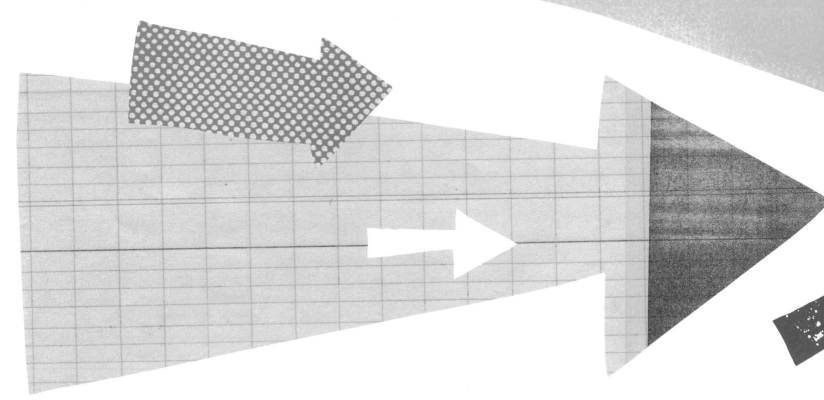

And that turned out to be ALL RIGHT, actually.
Although Mum wasn't too happy about her
car and the bike, she was pleased that
Arthur had told her The Truth.

So, what started out as a BAD day . . .

finished up being a **GOOD** day for Arthur.

And now Arthur
and The Truth are the
BEST of friends.

(And Arthur NEVER rode his brother's BIG bike again
– well, not anywhere near his mum's car!)

For George, Anna and Arthur – T. H.

For Grandma Gail x – D. T.

Bloomsbury Publishing, London, Oxford, New York, New Delhi and Sydney
First published in Great Britain in 2016 by Bloomsbury Publishing Plc
50 Bedford Square, London, WC1B 3DP

Text © Tim Hopgood 2016
Illustrations © David Tazzyman 2016
The moral rights of the author and illustrator have been asserted

A CIP catalogue record for this book is available from the British Library

ISBN 978 1 4088 6498 2 (HB)
ISBN 978 1 4088 6499 9 (PB)
ISBN 978 1 4088 6497 5 (eBook)

Printed in China by C & C Offset Printing Co Ltd, Shenzhen, Guangdong

1 3 5 7 9 10 8 6 4 2

All papers used by Bloomsbury Publishing are natural, recyclable products made from wood grown in well-managed forests.
The manufacturing processes conform to the environmental regulations of the country of origin.

www.bloomsbury.com